THE MASKED ONE

CONNOR WHITELEY

No part of this book may be reproduced in any form or by any electronic or mechanical means. Including information storage, and retrieval systems, without written permission from the author except for the use of brief quotations in a book review.

This book is NOT legal, professional, medical, financial or any type of official advice.

Any questions about the book, rights licensing, or to contact the author, please email connorwhiteley@connorwhiteley.net

Copyright © 2023 CONNOR WHITELEY

All rights reserved.

DEDICATION

Thank you to all my readers without you I couldn't do what I love.

CHAPTER 1

Professor Aleshia O'Kin truly loved exploring history, learning and telling everyone she could about it. In the Realm there were tens of thousands of years of history to explore, some of those thousands of years were home to such incredible cultures, others were home to people who showed Aleshia the sheer brutality of humans, and others still revealed how creative humankind was when faced with annihilation.

That was probably why she was obsessed with history before the Realm got formed and the kings and Queens and even a few Republics ruled over humans for the past few thousand years.

Aleshia smiled as she stared out over the massive expanses of desert as she stepped outside her little canvas tent in the middle of nowhere. The amazing smell of cooking bacon, mushrooms and much more expensive meats filled the air as the entire expeditionary team woke up and started cooking.

Aleshia could never be entirely sure what time

her people got up, but judging by the most amazing smells in the air, they had clearly gotten up early.

And that was what Aleshia flat out loved about them all, since her and her husband had left their awful jobs at the University of King George, they had actually had even more grant offers to sponsor their trips and plenty more interns had wanted to sign up.

People talking, joking and singing filled the air almost to remind Aleshia of that fact, even now she couldn't believe how popular she was amongst the History community.

She wasn't exactly sure how word had travelled so far of her and her husband's resignation after the incident with Mount Flame, her getting possessed and her almost causing the apocalypse, but it had. And it was only now Aleshia realised how many fans she had all over the Realm and even amongst the Elves and dwarves.

And what really surprised Aleshia about it all was how many peopled wanted to know the answer to one (or two) simple questions. Why did she do what she did? And what drove her?

Aleshia wasn't really sure what the answer now was, she used to travel the world and explore ancient cultures because she wanted to prove herself better than her extremely famous parents.

But now… she just wasn't sure?

Her answer was always something about her love for travelling, experiencing new things and just learning about the past, so she could help the present and protect the future.

She had no idea how true that was.

But as Aleshia felt the burning hot sun start to warm up her skin and sweat slowly started to roll down her back, she was really looking forward to the expedition starting today.

Aleshia wore her normal (well normal for desert wear) long loose-fitting and extremely breathable trousers, shirt and boots. Some people on the expedition had decided to go topless (or nude in the evening), but Aleshia wasn't that adventurous.

But as it was so hot, she didn't mind at all, and she was hoping that her husband would join in at some point, and then Aleshia would have to admire him.

She was looking forward to that!

After Aleshia and her husband, Charlian, had decided to quit their jobs at the University, they had spent two wonderful days engrossed in history books trying to find their next place to go.

Then they found the stories of The Masked One.

Aleshia was rather surprised Charlian didn't know too much about the Masked One and the culture the stories came from considering he had studied it whilst they were in their first year of dating.

The Ingnic were master crafts people who managed to thrive in the massive desert conditions in the central regions of the Realm four thousand years ago. They weren't nomadic people (that had really surprised Aleshia), the Ingnic had somehow managed to create an entire empire and have it endure for about two thousand years during war, famine and drought.

Aleshia had no idea how they had managed that, because originally the empire had started next to a lake. But that had dried up so quickly the empire was almost dead before it had even begun.

Logic would dictate the Ingnics would just move to another lake or body of water to survive. But they never did that. They somehow managed to find enough water to not only survive, but grow, thrive and developing one of the largest empires in Pre-Realm history.

There was even circumstantial evidence that the Ingnic Empire expanded as far north as the Orks which was on the northern boundary of the Realm, and as far as south as… well no one knew because more and more evidence kept turning up showing how massive the Empire used to be.

Aleshia didn't want to officially guess, but she had always wondered if the Ingnic Empire had been around three times larger than the Realm. Making it around the same size as the human, Elven and dwarfish Empires of today.

For some reason that realisation just scared Aleshia silly, because those people would have to have been extremely clever, resilient and resourceful to grow an Empire to that extent all from a silly little dried up lake.

But what really scared Aleshia was why did it

collapse after two thousand years?

Aleshia felt a shiver run down her spine as she wondered about the scary, horrifying tales of the Masked Ones. He (or she) was meant to be the so-called equivalent of the Angel of Death in Ingnic mythology, with him descending on the guilty, damned or doomed in the dead of night and killing them.

Yet the story that really interested Aleshia was one about a little Cult dedicated to the Masked One and foretold the End of Days for the Empire where the sky would burn bright red as the heavens launched an attack so large that it blocked out the sun and burnt the Empire in cleansing flame.

Aleshia had to admit it was full of the dramatic, but in her decades of experience exploring the history of the world, she had learnt more than once that even the most over the top stories sometimes had a nob of truth to them.

Aleshia was starting to get really, really excited now.

As the smell of bacon, mushrooms and other meats got more intense and Aleshia felt her mouth salivate at the possibility of breakfast, Aleshia knew she had to find out what had happened.

And that all started with the stories of the Masked One.

The idea of exploring them excited Aleshia more than she ever thought possible.

CHAPTER 2

Honourary Professor Charlian O'Kin almost loved history as much as his wife but unlike her, Charlian had always had a great appreciation for the power hierarchies of the Realm so he supposed his interests were a strange mix of the past and present.

And today was no different.

The sound of horses moaning, riding and stomping up and down the immense cobblestone road made Charlian focus on them as he leant against a wooden pub along the high street of the city.

In all honesty Charlian had never heard of such a place before, but somehow Aleshia had heard of it and sent him for their expedition. Charlian loved watching all the different people in their different heights, sizes and clothes walk around visiting each of the market stalls that lined the cobblestone street.

The most amazing smell of cedarwood, sea salt and some dwarfish spice that Charlian couldn't remember for the life of him what it was called filled the air as a large wagon rolled past.

Then another and another. Charlian was actually

surprised at how busy the city was, he was expecting the entire city to be quiet and rather like a dying settlement exactly like in the cultures he studied. But here he stood in a massive thriving city with more than enough trade to keep busy.

That was probably why it had whatever Aleshia wanted, Charlian had absolutely no idea whatsoever what Aleshia had ordered from a city a few miles away from the desert but he was excited to find out.

Aleshia had always had a rather maddening gift of finding the weirdest but most useful pieces of technology and magic to help them, Charlian would have loved to have the same ability, but he wasn't so gifted in that department. At least he more than made up for it in more… Marital areas.

After a few moments Charlian smiled as he looked up into the perfectly clear blue sky and saw a large dragon covered in shiny fiery orange scales circling the city. That was Octon and Charlian truly, truly loved her.

After fighting side by side with her for decades in the military, Charlian knew exactly what she was doing and especially after the last expedition with Aleshia getting possessed, Charlian was more than glad he had Octon by his side protecting him.

But at this current moment Charlian wasn't sure what she was doing, he had said she should go into the surrounding countryside and hunt some rabbit for herself. Yet clearly she felt the need to stay close just in case something went wrong.

Charlian didn't know if that was a good or bad thing, but he was willing to wait it out, and if there were any bad characters in the city Charlian liked to think his outfit of leather trousers, trench coat and boots would make him seem like a local.

+Ya see him yet boss+

Charlian jumped as Octon spoke softly into his mind, he hadn't been expecting that in the slightest.

Charlian looked up and shook his head.

Octon wasn't wrong though to question, according to Aleshia, Charlian was meant to be meeting a merchant friend of hers who was going to give them a small wooden crate of something special she had ordered, and she wasn't going to tell Charlian what it was until she had it.

He had wondered if this was somehow related to her possession by a man who wanted to destroy the Realm. But Charlian knew that saga was thankfully behind them.

So he had no idea what was in this small crate.

Then Charlian noticed everyone (but him) was standing to one side of the high street and standing at attention with their hands behind their backs in complete and utter silence.

Charlian did the same and he shook his head as a massive solid gold carriage travelled down the high street with four tall black horses leading the way.

Then the carriage stopped in front of him.

If Charlian hadn't studied the Realm's Barons and Baronesses and how they run their cities and regions before he met Aleshia he probably would have thought something silly like the carriage belonged to the King. But now Charlian knew a lot better and this belonged to the Baroness of the city.

The carriage opened and a meaty hand stretched up and gestured Charlian to come inside.

+Stay safe boss. I ain't attacking a Baroness for ya+

As much as Charlian knew Octon was joking, it still really wasn't a comforting thought.

Charlian went into the carriage and was immediately surprised at the large benches that were covered in the finest red silk he had ever seen or felt. They were extremely comfortable too and Charlian started to wonder if he would borrow one for the expedition (or just Aleshia).

The sound of a woman coughed made Charlian stare at a remarkably thin woman in golden battle armour. He had to admit she was attractive and rather on the young side to be a Baroness, but from history alone it was clear to Charlian never to underestimate a person because of their age.

Charlian almost fell forward as he felt the carriage start to move rather quickly out of the high street and out of the City.

"Baroness Coldatar," Charlian said bowing his head.

Coldatar smiled and pointed to something under Charlian's seat. He looked down and saw a small wooden crate, he picked it up.

He was about to open when he realised he really didn't want to go against Aleshia's wishes this early in the expedition.

"Thank you my Lady," Charlian said. "But my lady, may I ask why you're in battle armour?"

"You may," Coldatar said. "I am heading far south for a meeting with the other Southern Barons and Baronesses and even the King. There is trouble on our southern borders and we wish to stop it,"

Charlian nodded and he felt the carriage pull to a slow stop.

"Thank you my lady," Charlian said as he got back the carriage.

"Give your wife my hellos, blessings and good fortunes for me," Coldatar said as she shut the carriage door and the carriage dashed off.

As Charlian watched Octon start to descend towards him, he felt his stomach twist for some reason. It was no myth in the Realm that the trolls, goblins and all the other horrid creatures that lived south of the border were a massive problem that wanted to invade.

But it was a problem that the King had to travel down personally to deal with the threat of invasion. That was concerning.

The ground shook slightly as Octon landed and Charlian smiled at the stunning beauty of her, so he climbed on and made sure the small wooden crate was safely in his arms.

And as they flew off Charlian couldn't contain

his excitement of flying off to see his stunning wife once again.

But starting the expedition too.

This was going to be epic fun!

CHAPTER 3

As Aleshia stood with a massive plate of crispy delicious bacon, mushrooms and peas outside the massive canvas mess tent that the expedition had setup. She loved watching the massive orange dot of Octon get closer and closer.

That meant her stunning husband was coming home.

Aleshia loved the warm feeling of the sand that sent pulses up through her boots and up into the rest of her body. But the only problem was she already knew that the day was going to be extremely hot, it was only a few hours since dawn and it already hotter than the day before.

As expedition leader Aleshia knew she was going to have to have more safety briefings with her crew and made sure they definitely had enough water, she wasn't going to let anything happen to anyone.

In an ideal world she might be able to find out what the Ingnic Empire had used as a water supply, but given that was well over two thousand years ago since their fall, she really doubted that supply would even still be around.

But stranger things had happened in history.

Now that the massive dot of Octon was close to the expedition base, Aleshia felt her excitement grow at the idea of seeing her utterly stunning husband. She was really looking forward to kissing and loving and exploring the area with him.

As Octon landed with a thud revealing all of her majestic dragon beauty, Aleshia was half expecting the rest of the expedition crew to come out of the mess tent and help Charlian if he needed it. But they didn't. Aleshia couldn't moan at them for that, everyone knew they still had around ten minutes before the briefing and they still had to finish their breakfast.

So Aleshia finished off her delicious salty, meaty and just amazing breakfast, got a friend to wash up her plate and she went over to her handsome husband.

Aleshia hated the hot sand that had gotten into her boots but it didn't matter as she stared into the wonderfully warm eyes of Charlian. Aleshia had to admit he was just stunning in his new desert outfit.

Aleshia really wanted to run her hands all over his loose-fitting brown shirt, canvas trousers and boots, and judging by the trousers he was more than glad to see her.

Aleshia gave him and Octon a quick kiss and immediately took the small wooden crate from his hands. She was really looking forward to using it, and she was going to reveal what it was in just a moment when she did her meeting.

Needless to say what was in the crate was going to make long distance communication a lot, lot easier.

"You look handsome," Aleshia said giving her husband another firm kiss. She loved the feeling of his soft lips.

"Not so bad yourself. Might even do that whole nude thing tonight,"

Aleshia felt herself flush at that, she certainly wouldn't mind.

"I'm good too ya know," Octon said.

Aleshia gave Octon another kiss on the snout and smiled. "It's good to see you again,"

"Good to see ya too girly,"

"What's in the crate hun?" Charlian asked with an evil grin.

As much as Aleshia knew he would respect her wishes about not opening the crate, she did have to be sure. She didn't want to ruin the communication surprise.

"Did you?" she asked.

He shook his head. That made Aleshia feel great, it was amazing to know that after everything that had happened, he still trusted her to lead an expedition.

Aleshia smiled and turned around to face the mess tent, and for the first time in her expedition history everyone had already washed up their plates and bowls and cooking things. And they were all standing behind her waiting for her commands.

She was about to start when she felt the beads of sweat rolling down her forehead, cheeks and back. Aleshia couldn't have the crew sweating any more than necessary and wasting their precious water supply.

"Back in the mess tent everyone," Aleshia said smiling.

Everyone let out a massive breath as if they had all been hoping she would say that and they all went back inside.

They all quickly sat back down in the rows upon rows of wooden tables and benches and they were staring at Aleshia waiting for her to start.

"As you know everyone we are here to investigate the stories of the Masked One from the Ingnic Empire,"

Aleshia smiled at the sound of excitement as people whispered amongst themselves.

"We're seeking any of their settlements within a hundred mile radius of here. This was their base of power for over two thousand years. There should be some kind of ruins here for us to explore, but please note…"

Aleshia faded off for dramatic effect and some of the crew were actually on the edge of their seats.

"We are not seeking to look at already existing finds. So we were be going west of their temples, gardens and graveyard that were discovered by my parents,"

Aleshia was a little disappointed by the groans in the room.

Charlian stepped forward. "Instead we will become the famous finders of new exciting and groundbreaking ruins,"

That got everyone a lot more excited.

"Back in your tents, I have given each tent a plan and a map and a compass for you to head off into the distance to find something-"

A young man stood up and interrupted her. "But how will we talk to you when we've found something,"

Aleshia smiled. She had been waiting for someone to say that, granted she had actually paid the young man to speak up at that moment, but it certainly didn't kill the excitement growing in her.

So Aleshia placed the small wooden crate on one of the tables and opened it. Revealing tens beyond tens of bracelets covered in silver and black jewels.

Charlian walked over and gasped.

Aleshia held one up. "All of you will be carrying these bracelets. These have been freshly created by the King's Magic Council and through my university and palace connections I have gotten us permission to test these out for the King,"

Everyone went deadly silent.

"They work simply," Aleshia said, "everyone, you simply put them on and when you want to talk to me. You need to picture me in your mind and your bracelet will connect to my Master Bracelet and we can talk that way,"

Everyone smiled, jumped up and ran over to Aleshia. They were all just as excited as her.

Aleshia gave everyone a bracelet and simply let them all walk back to their tents to get ready to depart.

At the very bottom of the crate were two larger, blacker and much heavier bracelets, Aleshia put one on herself and she passed the other one to Charlian.

As she put them on, she felt tens of voices connect to her mind, before going silent and she knew that everything was working. Because what she didn't tell the others was that this allowed her to monitor their life signs, water levels and locations just in case something went wrong.

Aleshia and Charlian weren't going to let anything bad happen to any of their crew.

But until then, Aleshia couldn't help herself but jump up and down at the idea of her crew finding something.

Of course she and Charlian had to wait here for the time being to coordinate everything, but Aleshia couldn't wait for that to happen.

And she knew that something massive would be found.

CHAPTER 4

To non-history people this probably would have not been the most exciting thing in the world, but to Charlian and Aleshia, this was amazing. Charlian always loved the exciting wait before the action happened.

It might have been six hours since the teams went out into the desert but this was the best part. Not only because Charlian didn't have to do anything but because there was so much tension in the air.

For both Charlian and Aleshia knew at any second one of the teams could call in and everything would change. They both knew that something would be found and they had to be ready when that finally happened.

Charlian had betted with Aleshia two hours ago how much longer they were going to have to wait, he said two hours (which was now) and Aleshia said four. He really, really hoped he was right.

Over the past few hours, they had spoken a lot

about the history of the empire, what other cultures had influenced them and even guessed about the reason why the Ingnic Empire collapsed as strangely as it did. And this was where the couple differed massively.

Aleshia (for some strange reason) believed that the empire collapsed because it had grown far too large for its size, and it simply become too ineffective to govern itself, leading it to fracture into small empires and then one by one they collapsed.

At first glance that seemed perfectly reasonable and Charlian was more than likely going to agree with her, but the two of them were sat here alone for six hours, so they had more than enough time to suggest stupid things.

So Charlian was rather inclined to believe that the Masked One lead to the fall of the Empire, and that all the stories were true about him and his powers and even the Doomsday Cult was right.

Aleshia had flat out refused to believe it because whilst she acknowledged magic existed in the world, it was a massive stretch to believe a Masked One (or whatever he or she was in the magical world) actually slaughtered a massive empire.

As much as he wanted to argue with his beautiful sexy wife, Charlian had learnt long ago not to. It wasn't worth the effort and anyway, both of them were going to be proved right or wrong soon enough when their crew found something.

Which reminded Charlian of something a young

man had asked before he left with his team, he had asked Charlian why did he make sure he waited here and coordinate everything when Aleshia was more than capable of doing it herself.

It was actually an interesting question and Charlian always had an answer for the interns, and an answer for his wife. The intern answer was rather simple, he was co-leader of the expedition and he had to help run the crew, expedition and keep everyone safe.

But the answer for his wife was a lot more special. And this was the real reason for making sure he stayed behind.

If there was no one around then him and Aleshia could have a quick shag in the tents without being interrupted.

And when he had told Aleshia that answer in the first half an hour of the expedition he was expecting her to playfully hit him. Instead she grabbed him by the collar of his loose-fitting shirt and pulled him into the closest tent.

He wasn't going to argue.

Charlian stared at his stunning wife with her sexy trousers, shirts and boots as they both sat at a wooden table in the mess tent, and both did their own thing for a little while. Aleshia was reading through what she called her "back issues" of Realm Historical. In reality they were all the journals and magazines that the Realm Historical Association had published in-between their expeditions, and neither one of them read it regularly.

It sometimes became a problem because when they went to conferences, it was a nightmare and rather embarrassing when a famous person introduced themselves and neither one of them had any idea who they were. And everyone else knew them because they had read the magazine with their famous discovery included.

So that was why expeditions were so great. It gave both of them plenty of time for reading, loving and exploring the world.

Charlian kept staring and admiring his beautiful wife and every so often she blew him kisses as she sipped her tea. To normal people it might seem weird the entire thing, but after decades doing expeditions together, Charlian and Aleshia had learnt they didn't always need to be talking to be intimate with each other, and sometimes they just needed a bit of quiet time.

Which was extremely difficult to do when you have an entire crew surrounding you.

As a wonderfully cool breeze flew through the tent, Charlian hoped that Octon wasn't getting sun burnt out there. He had sent her to fly around the desert making sure all the crew were okay and didn't get into trouble. And thankfully there hadn't been.

Yet.

Aleshia smiled as she stood up and stretched her neck. "Believe me, I'm never studying Post-Unification History,"

Charlian could only nod at that. He didn't mind the twenty year unification war and the following eighty years where the various kings and Queens cemented their power and rule to form the Realm as it was known today.

But Aleshia had only ever been interested in what happened before the Realm.

"Oh I forgot to mention Baroness Coldatar wanted me to give you her hellos, blessings and good fortunes," Charlian said.

Aleshia laughed a little. "Thanks babe. That's just her little way of wishing me luck and wanting us to do well,"

Charlian nodded. "Anything good in the magazines?"

Aleshia sort of shook her head. "I would look through the magazine from two issues ago. They have some work on the Ingnic Empire and their territory in the current Elven lands, but besides from that nothing of extreme interest,"

He doubted his wife actually wanted him to have a read of that, but he was definitely going to after the expedition. That was rather interesting because that would be around the first ever historical mention of humans encountering elves and the following trade, conflict and celebrations that happened afterwards.

"Professors!" someone shouted.

Charlian and Aleshia both looked around but no one was there.

"Professors!" someone shouted as loud as they

could.

Charlian laughed as he pointed to the massive silver and black jewelled bracelets on their wrists.

He could actually see the embarrassment on Aleshia's face.

Aleshia tapped the bracelet. "Yes, professor Aleshia speaking,"

A young woman's voice got a lot clearer. "Professor Aleshia come to our location immediately,"

"Why?" Aleshia asked. "Do you need medical assistance?"

Charlian's stomach twisted at that sentence.

The young woman laughed. "No professor. Much better. We found something!"

CHAPTER 5

Aleshia could barely contain her excitement and her hands were physically shaking as her, Charlian and Octon flew towards the team that had apparently located something. She had no idea what they could have found but Aleshia really, really wanted to find out.

Her mind was spinning with all the amazing possibilities it could be, maybe they found a tomb, a temple or even a religious site where the Masked One was written about. That would be amazing and extremely helpful to Aleshia.

If she could find any mention of the Masked One then that could help her learn about the fall of the empire and start to fully understand what the point of the Masked One was within the empire.

And Aleshia loved the wonderful feeling of Charlian's strong arms wrap tightly around her, she loved being with him and that only caused her excitement to increase even more. She was really,

really looking forward to exploring with the man she loved.

Aleshia felt boiling hot beads of sweat roll down her back and start to dampen her loose-fitting shirt and trousers as they flew through the air. Aleshia couldn't believe how hot it was even this late in the afternoon, it wouldn't be too long until the sun started to set, but it was still boiling.

As more and more sand dunes and miles upon miles of sand flew under them, Aleshia was starting to understand what her crew was enduring. She hadn't realised the desert was this massive, if the crew returned tonight and commented on the journey then Aleshia would have to stop the expedition for a day or two and order some horses or extra dragons for her crew.

She wasn't having them risking their lives and dying because she hadn't realised how far she was asking them to travel.

In fact she might have to do that anyway just to make herself relax.

But what Aleshia did find odd was how the boiling hot air didn't smell of anything, it only smelt dry and deadly. She didn't want to spend too long out in the sun just in case she got dehydrated or something.

Because Aleshia had made sure to give the crew all the magic water bottles (endless canteen filled with cold water) that she had bought on the expedition. As much as she didn't regret it because the crew were always her priority over herself, she did wish for a bit of coldness about now.

As Aleshia felt Octon slow down a little and the sound of her wings flapping slowly came to her ears, she looked ahead and smiled as there was a massive sand dune with five little dots on top waving at them.

Aleshia's stomach filled with butterflies as her excitement shot up and her mind buzzed with all the amazing possibilities once more. She was really, really hoping it was going to be something about the Masked One.

Then she realised that all the little black dots on the dune were waving at Octon to stay put.

"What do ya wanna do boss?" Octon asked.

Aleshia felt Charlian rest his chin on her shoulder and that was enough for her to know that he wanted her to answer.

"Fly over there and let's see what they want," Aleshia said, more demanding than she wanted.

Octon zoomed over to the dune and as she hovered in the air, Aleshia smiled at the tall elegant woman who was the team leader and the four men around her.

"Report," Aleshia said.

The young woman smiled. "Professor, we'll slide down the dune. Then we need Octon to flap her wings and blow the dune away,"

Aleshia smiled. The young woman definitely knew how to make things sound interesting, and it sounded like there was something inside the dune itself.

And judging by the massive size of it, it had to be a grand temple or something.

But a few expeditions ago Aleshia had thought the same about a snow covered cliff face, Octon flapped it away and Aleshia was gutted that the snow only covered a small burial chamber for two people.

That hadn't been fun!

Aleshia kissed her husband and tapped his arms and he released her.

"Race to the bottom?" she asked as she slid off Octon.

She landed with a thud and the boiling hot sand was already going into her boots. Maybe this had been a very bad idea, but Aleshia was here now and she had to act like the wonderful fun leader she was known for.

"Go" the young woman shouted, sliding off.

Aleshia ran.

She jumped.

Aleshia slid down the dune.

Sand kicked up into the air.

Aleshia covered her eyes.

She kept sliding and sliding and sliding.

A full minute later she stopped and jumped up as she watched the young woman and her four male team members slid down behind her. Then Aleshia realised what had actually gone on and she felt extremely stupid.

The crew hadn't wanted to slide down first, they

had wanted Aleshia to go down, see if there was any hard rocks that would cause them to break a bone hidden under the sand. Then go down.

"Thanks for that," the young woman said with an evil grin.

Aleshia had been completely right, but she didn't mind considering how fun it was.

"Ready!" Charlian shouted as Octon flew back.

Aleshia ran back a little more and made sure the young woman and her teammates were behind her. Then she nodded to Charlian.

Octon rapidly flapped her wings.

Sand moved.

Sand kicked into the air.

Creating a sandstorm.

Something was moving.

Something was inside the sandstorm.

Octon kept flapping.

Then as the sandstorm cleared Aleshia screamed in utter delight as she stared at a massive granite pyramid. It was easily a hundred metres high and another four hundred metres wide.

It was stunningly beautiful with how the dark granite shone and even sparkled slightly in the sunlight. Then Aleshia saw a large black opening at the very bottom.

Aleshia had no idea what was inside. She didn't know if it was filled with sand, gold or even empty.

But she really wanted to find out.

She had to find out what happened.

And that really, really excited her.

CHAPTER 6

As Charlian kissed his amazing dragon goodbye and told her to wait outside, he followed Aleshia and the five crew members and went into the pyramid.

Thankfully Octon had lit up some torches for them, Charlian hadn't been too pleased with that idea because he really hated the heat so he didn't want another heat source so close to him, but they needed the torches to go inside the pyramid.

Charlian bagged out his already loose-fitting shirt and trousers as he held up the torch and gasped as he went further into the pyramid.

Everyone immediately came out into an immense chamber that seemed to be the only room in the entire pyramid, and Charlian couldn't believe how beautiful it was.

All the immensely tall walls were covered in a thin coloured layer of gold with millions of tiny symbols painted, carved and forced into it. Charlian had no idea how many words were in here, but from what little he knew about the Ingnic language, there was enough words in the pyramid to fill a library if they were converted to words.

But the smell was utterly disgusting. Normal people probably would have fled by now, but Charlian loved that old mouldy, musty history smell. It was the smell of true history and that they were walking in somewhere truly old.

He did have to admit though, he was forcing himself not to gag.

The sound of Aleshia laughing and jumping up and down in delight echoed as the crew members were talking amongst themselves. It was such a beautiful sight because they had actually discovered something.

Charlian went over to his stunning wife and hugged her. He immediately saw how thrilled she was with it all, and he was too. Most people would panic about the years maybe even decades it would take to decrypt the language and fully understand everything about the pyramid. But that didn't bother Charlian and Aleshia.

That was what they lived for.

Yet through the pitch darkness, Charlian thought he saw something reflecting the torch light so, he grabbed Aleshia's soft hand and led her over to the strange reflecting light.

Aleshia screamed as loud as she could in delight when they both saw a massive golden throne and even a coffin.

They both hurried over and then realised it was on a raised granite platform so Charlian pushed Aleshia up and she pulled him up.

They both stood in front of the coffin and was immediately taken by the size of it. It was made from solid gold and diamonds, but it was large enough to fit an entire family inside. It wasn't normal size in the slightest.

And what surprised Charlian was there were no inscriptions on the coffin. There was always, always at least a single word or image carved into the coffin to warn away evil spirits or stop the predations of the Masked One.

But this one didn't have anything like that.

The same was true for the rather larger golden throne that sat looking straight at the coffin. It was almost like there was meant to be a guardian sitting on the throne watching over the coffin.

Then Charlian felt his stomach tighten into a painful knot as he wondered what the guardian was watching for. To stop someone getting into the coffin or the much more alarming idea was did they want to stop anyone getting out.

That idea terrified Charlian. Especially if that person was still inside.

"What do you think was the point of this?" Charlian asked.

Aleshia shrugged as she focused on the coffin.

"I never knew the Ingnic empire not to protect their dead from the Masked One,"

Aleshia looked at him and cocked her head from side to side. "I'm not so sure about that. There is a lot of literature on the Masked One and the Ingnic funeral rites. But there was one rather scary article I read once…"

Charlian waited for a few seconds to pass before he gestures Aleshia should continue.

"Oh sorry," Aleshia said smiling, "I'm not wondering why there are diamonds on the coffins,"

"The scary article?" Charlian asked.

"Oh yea," Aleshia said, "the article was a piece done by a good scholar telling us about an inscription on a stone tablet that told us about the funeral rites and how to prepare the body of an Ingnic Warrior,"

Charlian nodded. "Oh I think I read that article. Wasn't it about a tablet that told how to prepare the body of a criminal warrior?"

Aleshia smiled and nodded. "Yes that was a later translation and that article was sadly a lot less publicised by the Association,"

Charlian was about to let that be it because they both knew how the article went, but then he heard the heavy breathing and purposeful coughing of five people behind them.

He looked and Aleshia and she was more than happy to continue. They both saw it as a chance for the crew teams to learn some more.

"But the tablet was discovered to detail how to prepare the body of a criminal as an offering to the Masked One," Aleshia said.

"That tablet is the only piece of evidence we have that sacrifices were made to the Masked One," Charlian said.

"But what did it say about the Masked One and why the bodies?" the young woman asked.

And thankfully Charlian remembered her name as Jessico Franklin.

Aleshia step forward and started waving her hands around as she spoke. Charlian knew from experience how deadly it was to stand next to her now.

"It didn't offer too much information because it was just an instruction set. But it did stress the importance of properly preparing the corpse and making sure not to spoil the liver, heart and brain as not to spoil the dinner to the Masked One,"

Charlian nodded. He had always thought of that as strange, but if these people believed that the Masked One could be kept happy. Then maybe it would help them learn more about it.

Then something clicked.

Charlian looked over to Aleshia who was leaning against the coffin and she shot back.

"What happened!" Charlian shouted.

Aleshia frowned. "I don't know. Something moved inside the coffin and the diamonds clicked,"

"You pressed the opening mechanism professor," Jesscio said.

Then the coffin opened.

Everyone's face went deadly white as the entire

coffin unfolded.

And fear gripped Charlian.

He knew never to open a coffin without the proper equipment.

It never ended well.

And they just had.

CHAPTER 7

Aleshia flat loved watching the utterly amazing golden and diamond coffin unfold before their very eyes inside the massive solid golden pyramid with its colourful gold walls covered in millions of breathtaking symbols.

It was so beautiful to Aleshia and she was really, really looking forward to exploring and learning and discovering every little thing she could about it and what it meant in terms of the Masked One.

When the coffin finished unfolding, Aleshia just laughed at Charlian's fearful expression and bright white eyes, he was clearly scared and she understood why. The unfolding coffin was beautiful and a real symbol that they were making progress.

Aleshia took a few steps closer to the coffin and frowned when she saw it was completely empty except a good number of bones. She picked up one of the bones and it was clear that they were all early human bones, maybe three thousand years old, which would place the pyramid in the middle of the Ingnic empire.

To normal people and the expedition crew that probably seemed crazy that she could tell the age of the bones just from looking, feeling and weighing them in her hands. But after decades of expeditions, Aleshia knew bones like the back of her hands.

Aleshia looked at Charlian and judging by his smile he had come to the same conclusions. This was amazing and a legendary find all by itself.

There were so few historical sites from around that time. Aleshia and Charlian and the crew were going to be famous for discovering this, but they did have to make their discovery a bit more concrete first.

Aleshia realised that they probably had an almost complete human skeleton here. Judging by the pelvis and the shape of the forehead it was clearly a man, probably around twenty years old judging by the teeth, but some of the bones were wrapped up in something crispy.

As Aleshia waved over the crew and pointed to the wrapped up things, she wished she had bought some of her personal equipment now. At least with that she would be able to photograph (using magic) some of the findings in their original site.

"Professor," Jesscio said, barely touching the wrappings.

Aleshia nodded.

"It feels wet and hard at the same time. Almost like these were dipped in something before the wrapping of the body," Jesscio said.

Charlian came over to Aleshia. "I think this is a sacrifice to the Masked One. I think they dipped the wrappings in a honey solution,"

Aleshia cocked her head at that for a moment. It made sense for the Ingnic people to dip the wrappings in honey because they never would have wanted the meat inside to go off before the Masked One could eat it.

Honey would definitely do the trick as it was already used as a medicine in the empire, and even now it is still used as an antibiotic.

But Aleshia didn't understand why the solution would go crispy and hard. She could clearly see the wrappings were crispy as Jesscio tapped on them. She just didn't know what caused it, especially as honey wouldn't dry out inside the coffin.

Charlian stood up and stretched his back.

"If this is a sacrifice," Aleshia said, "then where is everything else. The Ingnic normally buried their sacrifices with herbs, sweet treats and other offerings to the Masked One judging by the random texts that have been found,"

Jesscio carefully picked up one of the wrappings. "Professor, this material fills like parchment,"

"Like paper parchment?" Aleshia asked.

Jesscio nodded.

"Save that and take it back to camp please," Aleshia said. "When you get back prepare to the Boar solution and start the soaking process please,"

Jesscio nodded and started to wrap it up in some cloth that she got out of her bag.

Aleshia was rather curious about it because in the tiny amount of things that she had found and others had discovered about the empire, they never buried anyone even criminals with parchment. Everyone was buried naked or in cloth.

Aleshia started to feel her excitement build once more at the idea of finding something groundbreaking. If she was right and they had discovered something brand new from the empire, it would make herself, her crew and Charlian some of the most famous in the Historical Association.

But there were still so many questions about the coffin. It was clear that it was a sacrifice to the Masked One to make him or her not attack or claim anyone in the empire. That would definitely explain why there were no markings or symbols on the body or anywhere nearby to keep evil spirits away.

Charlian placed his wonderfully warm hand on Aleshia's shoulder. "This is a good find. Want to head back to camp and plan how we'll continue the investigation in here?"

Aleshia was about to say yes, that was certainly the only downside to these expeditions. It was all well and good finding things but then you had to organise how you were going to continue to study it.

It shouldn't have been too difficult considering Aleshia and Charlian had over 30 people here to help them. but Aleshia really didn't want to call everyone back just so they could study this massive pyramid.

Aleshia turned to face Jessico. "Can you stay here for the time being? Protect the site, keep exploring and start translating some of the symbols on the wall please?"

For a moment Aleshia thought she was going to say flat out no, but her entire team looked at each other and jumped up and down. They really wanted to stay here and start the amazing work on decrypting the pyramid's secrets.

Aleshia was actually jealous for them.

Charlian and Aleshia smiled at each other. They really wanted to be here too. To Aleshia there was still nothing better than exploring, discovering and retelling history with amazing other people who loved history just as much as her.

But there was still something wrong.

As much as Aleshia loved the finding of the sacrifice, it still didn't help her understand what the Masked One, its purpose and how the Ingnic empire collapsed as suddenly as it did.

Aleshia was no closer to finding out the truth, and that annoyed her.

But for some reason, she just knew that the next great discovery was just around the corner.

And that got her extremely excited.

CHAPTER 8

Even though the sun was starting to set in the distance creating massive pink and orange and red stripes in the desert sky, Charlian still couldn't believe how extremely hot it was back at camp.

He and Aleshia had considered getting the other teams to return and restart the search tomorrow, but Aleshia had somehow convinced him to let them search for another few hours and then Octon would go out and pick them up.

Charlian felt the far too hot sand slide into his boots as he and Aleshia sat in the large mess tent at camp. He was surprised how the evil heat of the day had started to cruelly heat up the wooden benches and tables, so whenever Charlian put his arms, legs and bum he sent pulses of warmth right into him.

But he wouldn't have it any other way considering what they had just discovered. Charlian was surprised to find the skeleton in the coffin wrapped up in parchment, and he was really hoping that the soaking process would allow them to unwrap the parchment and hopefully there would be some kind of writing inside.

Charlian didn't know what he was hoping for, but it made sense for the Ingnic empire to write prays, hymns or maybe something else entirely to please the Masked One when he eventually came across the sacrifice.

Charlian actually loved the calming sound of the silent camp with only the heavy breathing of Octon and Aleshia that broke the silence.

As Charlian stared at Aleshia who was sitting opposite him, taking deep breaths of the disgustingly dry and deadly air. He had to admit she looked so sexy and damn well beautiful in her stunning loose-fitting shirt, trousers and her face was so… perfect.

After a few hours in the desert, Charlian knew his face looked cracked, beaten up and just awful. But somehow Aleshia managed to look so stunningly beautiful.

Charlian was really, really looking forward to their alone time later on.

When Octon coughed a little, Charlian went to stand up to make sure she was okay but Octon nodded, and he sat back down.

It had been great flying back on Octon, especially as she went so fast it created more than enough wind to cool Charlian down. He loved that. And she was telling them tales of dragons, humans and even how the dragons had interacted with the Ingnic empire back in the day.

As Charlian understood it that was when dragons were in their infancy as far as history was concerned and they had only just started to seek out other species to trade, talk and investigate.

According to the dragons, the Ingnics were terrified of them at first because they, apparently, looked far too similar to the original tales of the Masked One.

When Octon had told Charlian and Aleshia that, both of them were more than a little surprised because there was a theory going round that the stories of the Masked One went through three major revamps through the two thousand years of the empire. Charlian had always believed it to be a bit of a myth, considering there was little evidence for it, but now he wasn't sure.

But he did trust Octon. So he believed her and the dragon stories.

That got Charlian thinking.

"What if what we found was from an earlier or even later set of stories?" Charlian asked Aleshia.

Aleshia opened her eyes and smiled. "That would make sense actually,"

Charlian stood up and went round the table to sit next to her. "Exactly. The current stories say that no sacrifices or rare ones were made to the Masked One,"

A chunk of wood snapped.

Part of the tent fell down.

Charlian turned around to see Octon trying to look innocent as she fixed the tent. Charlian knew she was just trying to fit into the tent and become part of the conversation.

He looked at Aleshia and gestured towards the door. Aleshia kissed him and they both went over to the door (more like an opening) of the mess tent and sat in the shade so Octon would feel more included.

"Thanks," Octon said. "I looked at the outside ya know when you were in it,"

Charlian smiled and leant forward. He had completely forgotten to check the outside of the pyramid for marks or symbols.

"And peeps there was the Ingnic symbol of the Second Age. What does that mean?"

Charlian looked and Aleshia and forced himself not to smile. It was an amazingly unpopular theory that proposed that the Ingnic empire divided itself into four different ages. Each one was as long as one of their Royal Families lived for, Charlian believed in the theory, Aleshia really didn't.

Aleshia went to open her mouth, but stopped.

Charlian rubbed her shoulder. "So that would place the temple around the midpoint in the Ingnic empire like you said,"

Aleshia nodded. "True. But when did our current stories about the Masked One come from?"

"Why that important girly?" Octon asked.

"Because," Charlian said, "if we can place our current stories were no sacrifices were made to the

Masked One. Then we have to estimate if these newer stories that influenced the temple and the coffin come before or after these stories,"

Charlian hadn't even noticed Aleshia had got up and picked up a textbook.

"This says our stories are from the beginning of the Empire," she said.

Charlian laughed a little in excitement. "Brilliant! That means we have found possible proof that these stories did evolve over time,"

Octon shook her head. "Ya boss. But if the empire changed tha stories to include protecting bods against him. Why did they become fearful of the Masked One?"

Charlian was about to respond when him and Aleshia just looked at each other.

They both knew exactly what Octon was implying. She was implying that the Masked One in all the stories wasn't a mythical equivalent of the Angel of Death, a punisher of the dammed and a protector of the good.

She was saying that the Masked One could be real. A living breathing person.

And that was enough to terrify the Ingnics.

The only question Charlian had was, should they still be scared two thousand years later?

CHAPTER 9

If it was any other time of the day Aleshia might have been annoyed at a late call, but just as Aleshia and her sexy husband had started to call everyone back to main camp, and even sent out Octon to pick them up. One of the teams had decided to call them and tell them about a brilliant new site they had discovered a few hours ago.

Aleshia had no idea whatsoever why the team didn't call it in earlier. That was what they were meant to do so she was not impressed in the slightest about that mistake of theirs, but they promised her over the silver bracelets that it was a good one.

So Aleshia was really hoping to be able to forgive them instantly.

When she told Charlian about it because he was making a start on dinner for everyone, he wasn't too impressed either because now he had started to make his famous (only to her) Onion Soup for all thirty crew members. He couldn't just stop for some theory.

Aleshia had to go alone.

And as cold as it sounded, she was really looking forward to that. Sometimes on expeditions, she did like a little alone time so she could just soak in and become absorbed into the historical sites without a rather handsome man distracting her.

Then Octon returned and Aleshia had decided to go out with her to inspect the new site that the team had found.

With the wonderfully warm wind whipping her long brown hair into a mess, Aleshia held onto Octon tighter as she slowed down and started to descend.

Aleshia wasn't impressed so far because all she could see was a small group of people blending in perfectly with the sand that seemed to stretch out for hundreds upon hundreds of miles. It didn't look like anything was here.

But that only got Aleshia more thrilled to be here. It meant there was something gripping and so special that the Ingnic felt the need to hide it!

When they softly landed Aleshia slid off her and Aleshia felt the soft sand move under her feet and she almost lost her balance. When she found it again, she looked at the massive smiling faces of a group of five middle-aged men who were looking far too pleased with themselves.

Aleshia didn't know too much about the team off the top of her head, she seemed to remember they were former interns and mature students, but she had never focused on them too much.

"Oh professor!" the youngest of the men said. He was clearly the leader and clearly excited about their discovery.

Aleshia decided to play it a bit harsher to make them work really hard to try and please her.

"Team leader I do not appreciate my crew hiding findings from me," Aleshia said coldly.

The Team Leader frowned. "Oh professor, I am sorry but I didn't want to waste your time. And I promise you I haven't,"

Now Aleshia was starting to remember him a little more, his name was Carl and just like he was now, Aleshia always remembered him as an eager student who always needed to be validated.

He was going to have to earn it today. Aleshia could have been back at camp working with her amazing husband and staring at his impressive ass as he cooked. But oh no, she was here instead.

"What it then lad?" Octon asked.

Aleshia smiled. Octon was right.

Then the group of men stepped to one side revealing a reasonably large opening to a cave made from granite. The opening was about the height of Aleshia.

"What is it?" Aleshia asked.

"Oh professor, you don't want me to spoil the surprise,"

Now Aleshia was really wishing she was back at the mess tent and camp helping her husband. But there was something in Carl's voice that made her know for a fact that there was something amazing inside.

Aleshia smiled and went towards the cave.

One of the other men got Octon to light up some torches and everyone went inside. Octon started shooting up fireballs into the sky for fun whilst she waited outside. Yet again.

As soon as Aleshia went inside, she was shocked to see air breath condense and how small the cave was. The cave only went back twenty metres and it was only five metres wide. This wasn't what she had been expecting.

And to make things even stranger, there was nothing on the smooth granite walls except five symbols that kept repeating.

Aleshia had seen the symbols before in countless stories of the Masked One but there were some subtle differences with these ones, and knowing the Ingnic language, they were differences that transformed the meaning of the words.

But Aleshia still had no idea whatsoever why the team took hours to call this in, what were they studying for that length of time?

Aleshia went deeper into the cave and the gagging smell of lemons, rotten meat and honey threatened to make her sick. It was such an awful concoction that Aleshia would have imagined to smell a lot better than it did.

Then she realised somehow the honey and lemons had gone mouldy and was only amplifying the smell of the rotten meat.

Aleshia held the torch lower to the ground to see if there was something on it to explain the smell. There wasn't. In fact the entire floor was made from solid smooth granite with a very disturbing pattern on it.

The floor was one big image of the Masked One. It was easily from the earliest part of the Ingnic empire judging by the snake-like tongue and feline whiskers that grew out of the snout. It looked awful.

But it was very clear that this cave was dedicated to the Masked One.

Aleshia was about to talk to the team and congratulate them when something wet, sticky and awful dripped onto her shoulder.

Aleshia looked up and gasped as there were five human skeletons nailed to the ceiling wrapped in parchment and dripping some strange honey and lemon mixture.

When Aleshia forced herself away to look at the team, she could only say one thing.

"Carl, tell Octon to get my husband. He needs to see this. Now!"

CHAPTER 10

When Charlian walked into the cave the first thing he noticed was the utterly disgusting smell of rotten flesh, lemons and honey. It was such a foul smell that Charlian just kept gagging until his nose somehow managed to find a way to deal with it.

It was the worst thing he had ever experienced.

After Charlian managed to make himself focus on the smooth granite cave itself, he smiled as he saw how stunning it was. He loved the amazing symbols that kept repeating themselves on the walls. Charlian knew that Aleshia wouldn't understand that, but he knew exactly what they said.

She was right about the little subtle differences like the swirls on the end of the symbols changing the meaning, but it was still easy to read if you knew what you were looking at.

Charlian felt his breath condense and the freezing cold air chilling his skin and he was instantly regretting not wearing something a lot longer and warmer.

Charlian felt Aleshia's wonderfully warm arms wrap around him from behind and she started to kiss his neck as he turned around to face her. Even though she had just discovered something horrific, Charlian couldn't deny how stunning she looked, and surprisingly happy.

Aleshia pointed up and Charlian gasped as he focused on the human corpses that were nailed to the ceiling. They looked horrific and like this was some strange sacrifice to demons and their demonic gods.

But the problem was the Ingnic never believed in demons or the darker side of the supernatural. This was strange to say the least. Moreso when Charlian considered that this cave was from the early part of the Empire, arguably when the Ingnic people were at their most logical.

Human sacrifices made no sense in most parts of the Ingnic empire, even more so in the earliest parts when religion, myth and folklore were extremely illegal and heavily enforced.

"What you make of it?" Charlian asked.

Aleshia shrugged. "Clearly something dedicated to the Masked One. There isn't anything in the historical records about sacrifices being made in the early parts, and then there's… that,"

Aleshia gestured up towards to the nailed human corpses on the ceiling.

But Charlian had a strange idea that might allow everything to start making more sense.

"Notice how these corpses aren't touched?" Charlian said.

Aleshia slowly nodded.

"Surely these corpses would be rotten and mostly destroyed after four thousand years in an environment that wasn't enclosed and protected," Charlian said.

Then Charlian heard the five men who were outside getting dinner from Octon come in. He really hope they were enjoying his amazing Onion Soup he had just finished making when Octon and Carl returned to collect him.

Aleshia nodded. "Yes. That does make sense. But why?"

Charlian smiled. "The throne,"

"The throne professor?" Carl asked.

Aleshia quickly explained to him and the other men what they had discovered in the pyramid and everyone's eyes were wide with delight. Everyone on the expedition was clearly hungry for the knowledge each discovery provided.

"So the throne," Charlian said, "is clearly something to do with it. And remember we didn't know what the point of it was,"

Aleshia gasped.

"I think," Charlian said, "the purpose is to attract, attack and contain the Masked One,"

Aleshia shook her head. "How? The throne was empty. The corpse inside the coffin was damaged and… you think the missing parts of the skeleton were eaten?"

Charlian slowly nodded. He didn't know if that was exactly what he was saying, but it was close. Very close.

The only thing that didn't make sense was what was on top of the throne. He believed strongly that it was a Guardian of sorts, but then if the Guardian was meant to attack the Masked One then why offer him gifts to…

Unless the Ingnic empire never wanted to please the Masked One. What if they wanted to kill it?

Aleshia was clearly thinking along the same lines. "I think we've been wrong about all this. The Ingnic were some of the cleverest and most logical people in the ancient world,"

Charlian threw his hands up in the air, she was right. Clearly Aleshia knew something he didn't.

"The Ingnic weren't the sort of people to willingly believe in myths and legends. And if we really get picky about the details, the stories of the Masked One only appeared after the first 100 years of the empire," Aleshia said.

"So?" Carl asked.

Charlian nodded. He wasn't sure either.

"So if they conquered, integrated or did something to another territory. Then it's most probable that those newly integrated people incorporated their stories into the empire,"

Charlian clicked his fingers. It made perfect sense, that example and mixing of beliefs was a common thread throughout history.

"And the Ingnic Royal Family wouldn't have such beliefs in the empire without there being a kernel of truth to them," Charlian said.

Then everyone in the cave went deadly silent.

"Then…" Aleshia said, "as the Masked One stories are featured for the next two thousand years…"

Charlian frowned. "What the hell did they find in these experiments?"

THE MASKED ONE

CHAPTER 11

That idea terrified Aleshia more than she wanted to admit, how the hell could the Ingnic empire set up some kind of experiment or trap to investigate the Masked One and find something.

That had to be impossible.

Aleshia wasn't going to believe it for a second, it was flat out impossible. It just had to be.

And if the experiments or traps were successful then why did the Ingnics not make that finding well-known. Why didn't someone else write it down, record it or just do something useful with the information.

Then again maybe they did, maybe modern day historians just hadn't found it yet. Aleshia knew that was a strong possibility.

With the smell of the rotten meat, honey and lemon getting stronger and stronger with each passing moment, Aleshia wanted to go outside for some fresh air, but she had to, she just had to find out what was going on here.

Aleshia turned to her amazing sexy Charlian and that needy Carl, who was being surprisingly tame today.

"Why and what did they find?" Aleshia asked looking at Charlian's stunning body.

Charlian pointed towards the five symbols that kept repeating on the cave's smooth granite walls.

"These symbols," he said, "they're talking about five results. I didn't fully understand it until now, but now I think I know what it says,"

Aleshia and Carl gestured him to continue.

"These results explain what happened in each of the five experiments. One for each body,"

Aleshia gasped. That was disgusting, how could these people conduct five experiments in this cave alone just to find out if the Masked One myths were true.

"The first three results varied in tiny ways that we wouldn't bother too much with today. They died normally without any supernatural interference," Charlian said.

Aleshia was amazed at how methodological and precise the Ingnics were, they probably recorded the exact time (down to the last second) each person died, and they probably didn't even have a term like natural causes. They probably explained each and every cause of death when someone died.

Aleshia both loved and hated that much precision.

"Want to know about the next two?" Charlian asked.

Aleshia nodded. She hadn't realised she was so lost in her own thoughts.

"The fourth person died violently. They kept screaming about a demon or something clouding their mind. They were screaming about being eaten. They were screaming that a Masked cat was mauling them,"

Aleshia's blood ran cold. That was graphic and awful, she almost felt sorry for these men. But surely there was another explanation for it, maybe the person was just crazy, insane or maybe the note taker made it up to scare the Royal Family?

Aleshia doubted it.

"Oh professor," Carl said, "the fifth?"

Charlian smiled. "Oh I miss translated this at first glance. I thought it was talking about a man who killed himself because the pressure was too much. But a Guardian angel killed him instead…"

Aleshia cocked her head at the idea of another Guardian comment. She didn't think it could be the same Guardian who was meant to sit on the throne in the pyramid, but she couldn't be sure?

But why had Charlian trailed off like that?

"Carl," Charlian said, "have you got a knife on you?"

Carl smile. "Oh of course professor,"

Charlian took the knife and jumped up. Forcing the knife into one of the people nailed onto the ceiling.

The knife went straight through.

Charlian smiled and laughed and it took Aleshia a moment to realise what was happening. Then she saw that the person Charlian had theoretically stabbed, wasn't a person. There was no one in the wrappings, but the person who made the wrappings did an amazing job at making it look like there was.

Aleshia just looked at Charlian. "Explain?"

"Oh professor," Carl said, "that fifth man wasn't buried here. He is buried in the coffin,"

Charlian frowned and nodded. Aleshia wasn't going to be praising Carl any time soon.

Yet it was strange. It was strange that the fifth man would be an experiment and then buried in the coffin with a fake corpse-looking thing nailed to the ceiling. It didn't make sense.

Charlian clicked his fingers. "They were doing a double-blind study!"

Aleshia's mouth dropped at the sheer intelligence it showed the Ingnics possessing. Double blind studies were when amazing experimenters didn't know who was in each group, so in this absolutely brilliant case, the experimenters didn't know where the real body was.

The body would have been in the coffin or nailed to the ceiling.

It was truly brilliant. And it showed Aleshia exactly what she wanted to know, the Ingnics clearly thought someone might try to fake the results of the study, so they wanted to make sure the chance of that was almost zero.

Aleshia couldn't believe that this was probably the earliest mention of this type of study in history. That alone was major! Charlian was clearly pleased too.

Her excitement built and built. All Aleshia really wanted to do now was head back to camp and check out the wrapped pieces of flesh from the coffin to make sure.

Maybe that would only increase her confidence and provide some evidence for her idea.

But then she realised something just before Carl said the exact same thing.

"Oh professors!" Carl shouted, "so that means the Ingnics had wanted to study the Masked One. Then why were some of the bones missing from the coffin?"

Aleshia and Charlian both stopped their happiness and fear gripped them. That was what the Ingnics had discovered.

They were clearly expecting all the bodies to be okay and not attacked or eaten. But the one body they had covered in sweet sticky mixtures for the Masked One to devour had been eaten.

That body had been attacked. Aleshia had seen it with her own eyes.

No wonder the Ingnics were scared. They had proven that the Masked One was alive.

And that terrified Aleshia more than she ever wanted to admit.

CHAPTER 12

Charlian flat loved the next part.

Now the amazing parchment had been soaking for hours in a special solution, it was now soft enough to carefully unfold and reveal its stunning secrets to them all. But it was still more than hard enough to stop it breaking, ripping and dissolving in the solution.

As Jesscio and Carl bought out the two bowls containing the parchment out into the mess tent and onto the hot wooden table where Charlian and sexy Aleshia were sitting. Charlian felt his stomach get more and more excited at the amazing stuff they were going to find.

A few decades ago Charlian had done this exact thing on screwed up manuscripts that were twenty thousand years old. It was an agonising process but considering Charlian had been the first ever person to read that particular culture's stories, it felt like such an honour to Charlian, and more than wanted (he really,

really wanted) to have that honour again.

With the flickering light of the candles, torches and the little fires that were littered around the camp, Charlian was impressed that the mess tent was more or less fully lit. That was perfect for doing this sort of work, he never wanted to try this in the dark.

Aleshia kissed him as she handed him what could only be described as massive tweezes and a pair of bright white gloves. He knew they weren't going to be that colour when they were done, but as a past mentor had said to him, *the dirtier the gloves, the better the work*.

Charlian had no idea how true that was, but he liked to think it was.

When Jessico and Carl sat opposite to them, Charlian was surprised to see them so smiley and happy considering Aleshia had firmly said to them, they were NOT to touch the parchment.

Charlian gently pulled over a bowl containing the massive parcel of wrapped up parchment and he forced his stomach to relax.

He picked up the tweezes and started to extremely carefully pick apart the parchment.

Charlian wasn't exactly sure what to expect but considering this was the parchment from the fifth victim of the double blind study. He would have imagined some kind of medical record, words of scripture or just something to prove that the Masked One was alive and real.

It still terrified Charlian that that could even be a

possibility.

He hated to imagine how scared the logical and very rational Ingnic people were when they found out about it.

After a few minutes of picking at it, Charlian smiled as he found an edge of the parchment. Then he slowly started to work his way across the edge, unpicking it as he went.

To normal people and very early history students, this would have seemed like the most nitpicky job in the entire world, but it was critical.

You never ever could rush this sort of work. If you went too quick then the entire parchment or manuscript or whatever you were working on could and would just fall apart.

He had seen that plenty of times. And each time it happened Charlian just wanted to cry inside. It was like burning away entire sections of history just because someone wasn't patient enough.

"Where's Octon?" Jesscio asked.

Charlian took a deep breath of the dry sandy air, carefully placed his tweezes down and just looked at her.

"Please don't talk when we're doing this sort of work," Charlian said, "but she's looking for a missing team that hasn't responded to our calls on the bracelets,"

Aleshia sighed.

Jesscio and Carl nodded their respects and left Charlian knew exactly why Aleshia had sighed, at first when he first met her, he thought it was rude as hell for her to do that.

But after studying history and how it worked, he now understood. He was just a tat more respectful in telling people to go away.

Yet he would be lying if the whole missing team and Octon situation didn't bother him. He was amazed at how well the silver bracelets were working.

Charlian had spoken so easily to the crew over such vast distances. He didn't even need to be able to see them to talk to them. It was flat out amazing.

But this one team hadn't returned when they were called. And each time Aleshia called them, they physically stopped the call.

So Aleshia, as expedition leader, looked up their location (only Charlian and Aleshia knew she could do that) and sent Octon after them. By now Charlian had expected to hear from her or at least have her fly back, but there was nothing.

Charlian just wanted his amazing fiery orange dragon to be okay. He didn't think he could live with himself if anything happened to her.

As soon as him and Aleshia finished this, he had, just had to go and look for her if she wasn't back.

After ten more minutes, Charlian was almost shaking with excitement as he had managed to unpick a third of a page. He couldn't make out the parchment and its letters so far but that was normal.

Normally you need to unpick the entire wrappings or whatever you were doing, let it dry and then start the translation process.

It sounded long winded but Charlian loved it.

"Stop," Aleshia softly said.

Charlian blew her a kiss as he slowly stopped his unpicking and took out his tweezes to look at her.

Aleshia was smiling and when Charlian looked down at her bowl he understood. Somehow she had managed to unpick the entire thing and inside her bowl were five pages of something, some sticky mixture and some bones.

"Jessico! Carl!" Charlian shouted.

The two team leaders ran back in.

"We need wire racks, drying tables and… a magic heat lamp please," Charlian said.

The two team leaders ran off. Charlian just looked at what Aleshia had found. The pages were so beautiful, but Aleshia was focusing on the bones.

When the two team leaders returned, they placed two wire racks, the drying tables and a heat lamp on the table and Charlian slowly placed the five pages on the drying tables and turned on the heat lamp.

He wasn't sure how needed the heat lamp actually was considering they were in a desert and strangely enough it was boiling hot considering it was night-time. But they just needed these things dried out carefully and very quickly.

Aleshia carefully placed the bones on the wire racks and let the sticky mixture drip onto the wooden table below. They needed to get some more trays for their next expedition, that was a must.

"Feel this," Aleshia said.

Charlian picked up a small shin bone. It was a lot smaller than he expected considering the size of the rest of the skeleton they found.

Then he saw the bite marks.

"Oh," Charlian said, "this isn't the entire bone. What do you make of these markings, Carl?"

From what Charlian knew about the team leader, he was really interested in prehistorical creatures. So hopefully Charlian could find that a creature and not the Masked One made the bite marks.

Carl took the bones and cocked his head. "Definitely carnivore,"

Even Charlian could have guessed that. A plant eater was hardly going to eat a human in a coffin.

Carl smelt the bone and even licked it a little.

"That sticky mixture wasn't from the honey, lemons or rotting of the body," Carl said.

Charlian leant closer. "What was it?"

Carl smiled. "It's from the first ever race of dragons. The Megaragons,"

Charlian felt his heart stop for a moment as fear gripped him.

Those creatures were rageful, ruthless hunters that killed entire populations.

But what really concerned him was, Megaragons were meant to have died out over a hundred thousand years ago.

But the start of the Ingnic empire was only four thousand years ago?

So the real question, that terrified Charlian was, was if a Megaragon could survive 96 thousand years past its so-called death.

Could one still be alive now?

CHAPTER 13

These were some of the most amazing findings Aleshia had ever heard!

She was stunned that she was going to have the absolute honour of finding out more about these stunning creatures. Aleshia had heard of Megaragons in extremely old history books. Not a lot was known about them. But she was about to find out more about these stunning creatures.

This alone might be able to make her famous!

And it might be able to help her learn about why the Ingnic Empire fell as strangely as it did!

"So what are these Megaragons?" Jesscio asked to Carl.

Carl returned to Aleshia. "Oh professors, you must know what they are,"

At first Aleshia just thought he was being rude, then she realised he honestly didn't know enough about them to teach someone else.

Aleshia just gave him a fake smile. "Back two

hundred thousand years old in the far, far, far South. There were these dragon-like creatures,"

Jesscio leant closer.

"These creatures were massive. It meant mountain size or at least hill size. The fossil record is a bit touch and go on them, but we say the average size of them is about a hundred metres long,"

Charlian just shook his head. Aleshia wasn't going to disagree with him, they were massive!

"Then the fossil record shows the Megaragons started to move north and north and north. Until they reached where the very bottom of the Ingnic Empire would have been,"

Carl nodded like he knew all this already. Aleshia just wanted to hit him.

"After a while, the fossil records and the historical digs started to turn up a lot more messed up stuff," Aleshia said with a brave smile, "the digs turned up hundreds of Megaragons fossils but there was a twist in the tale,"

Charlian placed his head in his hands and Aleshia wanted to do the same. She had vomited the first time she heard it.

"Inside the Megaragon fossils," Aleshia said, "were entire populations of other animals. We're talking hundreds of sheep-like creatures, horse-like ones and every living thing was inside their stomachs,"

Charlian nodded. "And all tests show these animals were somehow alive when the Megaragon died but they were extremely weak,"

Aleshia shuddered. "Like the Megaragons eat them, kept them alive inside them and slowly drained the life force out of them to sustain themselves,"

That was the part Aleshia hated.

Carl nodded and Aleshia knew he was trying his best to suppress his shock and surprise.

"Oh professors that is exactly what I would have said,"

How Aleshia didn't hit him she didn't know.

Charlian stood up and stretched his back. "So how do you know that mixture came from those creatures?"

Carl smiled like he was a world-leading expert on the topic. Whatever he said Aleshia was definitely going to double check with a real expert before she and Charlian submitted her paper on the expedition and the Ingnic Empire

"My mentor before I signed up on the expedition was Dr Douglas McCall,"

As he continued, Aleshia forced her mouth not to drop open. Dr Douglas was… one of the best historians in the entire Realm. She knew him from growing up, he was taught by her parents so Dr Douglas certainly knew his stuff.

She just couldn't believe that Douglas would accept someone like Carl under their wings. Hell, Aleshia didn't want him but the more people he had the more grant money she was given.

"… So it was the taste that the chemical reactions

in their bones," Carl said.

Aleshia hadn't heard everything but she had heard enough. Those bite marks were definitely from these Megaragon creatures, but it was just strange how one had survived.

But then again that was the strange thing about the fossil record. It wasn't like a data system that always updated, it only got filled up when fossils were found.

So in all honesty, Aleshia knew for sure that a small colony of the Megaragons could have lived on and moved further up north to this area without any fossils being found.

Aleshia would love it if they found a fossil. That alone would send ripples through the Historical Association, but she added that to everything else they had discovered on the expedition already. Aleshia was basically going to be rewriting the known history books.

Well, a girl could certainly dream.

When she heard Carl and Jesscio laughing and looking so pleased with themselves for helping with a major breakthrough, Aleshia clicked her fingers and they both sat down.

Charlian just looked at her.

"So we know the sticky mixture and the bite marks and probably where the rest of the shin bone went," Aleshia said, "but we do not know or have any proof of the Megaragons being alive,"

Carl went to open his mouth but Aleshia stared

at him, shooting him a warning look.

She was serious now. She wasn't going to let one detail and, quite frankly, one massive guess give her enemies at the Historical Association a reason to laugh at her, her husband and dismiss her expedition as a joke.

Aleshia and Charlian had worked far too hard for that to happen!

Then Aleshia felt something vibrate on the wooden table inside the mess tent, she looked around but nothing else was moving. The canvas tent was gently moving in the warm breeze that was blowing through.

But nothing else was moving.

"You okay?" Charlian asked.

Aleshia looked around. The vibrations only seemed to get louder.

Charlian jumped and held his head.

Aleshia grabbed him.

Then Charlian started laughing and just looked at Aleshia. She didn't know why he was looking at her like that.

"Octon just mind sent me something very rude," Charlian said laughing.

Aleshia smiled. "What?"

"Answer your f-ing bracelet," Charlian said and gave her a kiss.

Aleshia felt so silly as now she knew exactly what was vibrating. It was her silver bracelet that allowed her to communicate with everyone.

She tapped it.

"Come now!" someone shouted.

"Why?" Aleshia asked.

"We found something injured. Something like a dragon. We need help. We need your expertise!" someone shouted.

A deafening roar ripped through the bracelet.

Then the connection went dead.

Aleshia thought her heart was about to explode out of her chest.

Aleshia knew what was happening.

The missing team had just found a Megaragon.

CHAPTER 14

Charlian's head still hurt a little from when Octon had shouted into his mind. But he flat out couldn't believe that the missing team had found something injured and that this thing looked like a dragon.

He was never ever going to admit or even think it was a Megaragon. That was ridiculous and he was actually surprised that Aleshia had thought that.

Charlian was going to need some hard evidence before he even started to believe that silly idea.

When Octon started to flap slower and Charlian felt an awfully hot breeze in the hot desert, Charlian wasn't sure what she was slowing down for, but then he noticed that the desert just dropped away all of a sudden.

Octon landed and Charlian gripped Aleshia's tight as the hot sand moved under the dragon's feet. Then Charlian slid off and helped beautiful Aleshia down (even in the pitch darkness of the desert he was still amazed how damn hot she looked), and he looked around.

It took his eyes a few seconds to adjust to the darkness but the slight glow of Octon's fiery orange scales was a great help. Charlian realised that all the sand was slowly moving towards something.

Charlian and Aleshia followed it and Octon slowly walked next to them. He wasn't sure if he could ever say that a dragon walked but he didn't know how to describe it, besides stomping.

Aleshia kept walking then Charlian saw the edge of the sand. He grabbed her. Pulling her close.

A few moments later Charlian's brain caught up with his eyes and he realised that the sand didn't end. It went down. The entire desert fell into a crater of sorts.

Charlian couldn't believe how massive it was. The crater was easily the size of a football pitch or maybe even ten. It was absolutely massive.

Aleshia started waving to something and Charlian's eyes narrowed as he saw at the very bottom was a group of humans and something massive, black and shiny.

His heart stopped for a moment at the idea of that being a Megaragon. Charlian turned to Octon who was smiling.

"So boss what do ya think?" Octon said.

Charlian wanted to dismiss the entire thing, but of course Octon had actually been down there to talk to the expedition crew.

"What is it?" Charlian asked.

He could see Aleshia getting excited next to him.

"It's… I donno boss. A massive dragon. Ten times bigger than little old me,"

Charlian looked down into the crater. She wasn't wrong, whatever that black thing was, it was extremely big. He doubted that if Octon flew down there he would be able to see her so clearly.

"You must have been down there," Charlian said.

Octon's smile deepened. "Yea boss. But… it strange. It ain't normal,"

Aleshia just looked at Charlian. "I think she wants us to go down there,"

Charlian went to open his mouth, but he didn't. He Knew that both Octon and Aleshia wanted to go down there but he didn't.

He didn't know why he didn't.

But it was probably because if they did find a Megaragon down there, then Charlian and his damn hot wife and his dragon best friend would be so close to a creature that could and would easily kill them all.

He just couldn't allow anything to happen to them.

CHAPTER 15

Aleshia was extremely, extremely excited!

When Octon flew down to the bottom of the crater and Aleshia and Charlian slid off, the first thing Aleshia noticed was the awful smell.

The entire crater stunk of rotten meat, lemons and honey. It was such an extremely awful combination that Aleshia just wanted to vomit and leave. It took all her strength not to gag in front of everyone.

But the sheer size of the sand crater was just amazing. Aleshia was just stunned by how it happened and was formed, it must have taken… she didn't know. Maybe it was formed by weather processes, a historical battle or maybe, just maybe a massive impact.

Something the size of a Megaragon smashing into the desert.

Then Aleshia walked over to the five crew members that were missing. They were all tall rather beautiful women that Aleshia had handpicked from her old university, they were all amazing people. So Aleshia wanted to give them the benefit of the doubt, she knew they had a reason for not calling her sooner.

Aleshia stopped in front of them and all the women just smiled at her and pointed to Aleshia's left.

She had no idea what they were pointing at but when Aleshia looked, she was horrified. There was a massive (and she meant fucking massive) dragon skull.

It was perfectly intact with eyes the size of houses, dagger-like teeth three times the size of Charlian. The entire skull was easily the height of the crater.

Aleshia just couldn't believe the scale of the creature. It was clearly massive, but there was one thing that she couldn't understand. When the team called her they said the creature was injured, and some reason the bracelet communication went silent.

She believed they were in trouble, but they all looked okay.

Charlian walked over and stopped next to her and judging by his head, he thought the same. It was strange that the team implied the creature was still living but here at Aleshia's feet was a massive skull.

Whatever the skull belonged to had clearly died thousands of years ago but without getting more advanced equipment from a sponsor or a university, Aleshia couldn't know the exact age for a while.

Before this Aleshia had always considered herself rather good at dating bones, but there was no chance in hell she was going to be able to feel, weigh and smell the bones. And she was great at dating human bones, not potential Megaragon bones.

"What do you think?" Charlian asked.

Aleshia turned around to face the women. "Why aren't you talking?"

The tallest and most poshly dressed of the group walked forward, clearly the team leader. "Cos Aleshia, we don't know what it is. We're too stunned!"

Aleshia could definitely understand that. Even with all her experience she had to make her brain not panic about what this skull potentially was.

"Did you just find it like this?" Aleshia asked.

"Yea," the team leader said, "we just walking like ya do. Shirley over there tripped over some bone. We follow it. Sand came out from under us. We fell down and found… that,"

The team leader pointed back to the massive skull. But it was strange how they made this… place sound hallow and like the skull created… a cave all by itself.

Aleshia wasn't sure if she believed it but it did make sense. If the Megaragon died, over thousands of years it would get covered in sand and it would get pressed down under the soil.

Then as the body started to fossilise or rot, the body would start to release gases and Aleshia already knew they produced a strange mixture of honey, lemons and rotten meat. So maybe that's what happened here.

Charlian tapped her on the shoulder, and Aleshia instantly knew from the look in his amazing eyes that he was thinking the same thing. She loved that about him!

"So," Charlian said, "we are thinking that the gases created by a massive body rotting created a… cave or underground chamber of some sort,"

Aleshia didn't know what to believe but it made sense. Especially when she did what she was best at. She was amazing at remembering history.

"Of course," Aleshia said, "studies estimate that this desert is twenty thousand years old. In historical terms that meant and from everything I know only one single culture lived and build something on this stretch of land in those years,"

"The Ingnics," the women said.

Aleshia nodded. "No one else in history has a culture built on this. Meaning no one was here to disrupt the gas created chamber,"

"Except the Ingnics," Charlian pointed out.

Aleshia wished she had an answer for him. Then she focused back on the massive skull and she noticed something. She noticed around the end of the snout there was twenty little holes.

And if she remembered the fossil record correctly from Megaragon studies, they all had little holes at the end of the snout for a very special function.

For whiskers.

Aleshia clicked her fingers. "Remember the floor of the cave we discovered,"

Charlian nodded. "Yea. It had a snake-like picture of the Masked One and it had whis…"

Charlian jumped up in the air and screamed in delight. Aleshia did the same.

This Megaragon was the exact match for the painting on the floor of the cave, because in all history books when dragons were first encountered by other races. They all (without fail) called them Flying-Snakes at first.

No one called them Dragons. Everyone called them Flying-Snakes.

Clearly the Ingnic Empire did the same and they must have become fearful at the sight of them and after they conquered or integrated a culture with the stories of the Masked One. That mythical creature merged with the Ingnic Empire's beliefs about that Flying-Snakes.

Aleshia was thrilled. This was amazing!

But there was one more thing she had to check.

She had to get her proof before she called these ideas as fact, or at least a scientific theory.

She had looked at the parchment pages of that wrapping.

Aleshia hoped, beyond hope that could provide her with some evidence.

But these massive Megaragon skeletons was amazing!

CHAPTER 16

By the time Octon flew Charlian, Aleshia and the expedition team back to the camp, it was already the early hours of the next day and if Charlian narrowed his eyes just enough then he could see a very thin line on the horizon.

He guessed in less than half an hour the pitch black sky would be burnt away and replaced with massive pink, red and yellow streaks as the sun shone up.

Charlian felt extremely tired and he just wanted to sleep, but he had to find out the truth. He had to confirm Aleshia's crazy theory. It was his theory too but he had to confirm it.

So Charlian and Aleshia rushed into the canvas mess tent where they were amazed some of the crew were still up playing cards and they went to the drying racks.

Charlian instantly smiled when he saw the five pages of parchment that Aleshia had unpicked earlier were perfectly dry. He knew he shouldn't really be too surprised given it was the dead of night and he was still sweating, but it was great news.

Charlian and Aleshia sat down on the warm wooden benches and their smiles deepened when they realised that some amazing crew members had unpicked Charlian's parchment when they were away.

Charlian looked around and noticed the crew playing cards were Jesscio, Carl and their own crews.

"Thank you!" Charlian shouted, maybe a bit more emotional than he intended.

But it just showed him how amazing these people were and that was why he and Aleshia had picked them. Everyone loved history here and they were all willing to work hard.

But what really struck Charlian was how great these pages of parchment were, he had seen plenty in all his years married and dating Aleshia. But never had they been in as perfect condition as this.

Charlian could probably read every single tiny word and symbol and image on them if he had a magnifying glass.

He had never been able to think or say that before. And him and Aleshia had studied hundreds, if not thousands, of historical documents between them.

"Let's see what we have here," Aleshia said to herself as she grabbed a magnifying glass from one of the benches. It must have belonged to a crew member.

Charlian leant over her shoulder and loved how wonderful she smelt despite the heat and the sweat he was feeling.

"Look," Aleshia said as she pointed to some of the pages.

Charlian slowly pulled over the drying rack and gasped at how beautiful the pieces of parchment were. He knew they had dried well, but the page that Aleshia was pointing to was decorated so well.

But the most interesting thing about it was a massive drawing of a snake eating its own tail with shades of blue, pink and blood red.

"See what I mean," Aleshia said.

Charlian nodded. In Ingnic culture, the symbol of the snake eating itself was legendary. It was a warning of sorts that Charlian always told others about because it was so applicable to the Realm today.

The symbol wasn't so much about consuming and eating yourself as part of cannibalism. The real point of the symbol was to warn people against putting yourself before others and not protecting the interests of your people.

It was theorised (but Charlian doubted it a little) that the Ingnic Empire always fall because the Royal Family would always consume itself by overindulging in its influence, power and resources.

Then Charlian realised that wasn't what Aleshia had been pointing at.

"See," Aleshia said pointing to the snout of the snake.

It was only then that Charlian realised that this wasn't a snake that had been eating itself. It was a depiction of the Megaragon and the Masked One.

Two creatures in myth.

One creature in reality.

And then Charlian knew that they were right. Him and Aleshia would still need to reread all the historical textbooks to double check how their new findings connected to the wider literature on the Ingnic Empire.

And they needed to finish reading all the gripping pages of the parchment.

But they knew they were right.

Charlian and Aleshia just looked at each other, smiled and laughed.

This was exactly why they were historians and loved exploring history. Because they wanted to spend all night exploring, discovering and improving their knowledge of the past.

And tonight they were definitely going to be doing that.

And Charlian couldn't wait. This was going to be amazing!

CHAPTER 17

As Charlian leant against his amazing wonderful dragon Octon, he just felt so amazing after last night. Sure him and Aleshia hadn't gotten up til lunch time, but it had been worth it.

Charlian loved the wonderfully warm feeling of the soft sand under his feet as he simply stood there waiting for Aleshia to finish getting changed in their tent before she came out to the mess tent.

Even after the crazy twenty-four hours, Charlian still loved every little thing about the expedition. Even the massive canvas mess tent where everyone was thankfully underneath in the cool shade finishing off their lunch.

Charlian was more than happy that everyone was in the cool shade and not risking their lives in the killer heat. It was actually worse than yesterday, if the expedition wasn't basically done, Charlian definitely would have called off today.

It was just far, far, far too dangerous to have the

crew wandering around in the desert, even with the silver bracelets that allowed them to monitor their life signs.

A wonderfully cool breeze washed over the camp Charlian just smiled at how good it felt to have a moment of coolness in amongst the heat. The breeze even smelt beautiful with its hints of moisture, flowers and damp.

After all the extreme heat and the killer temperatures last night, Charlian didn't want that breeze to end, and even the smell got him excited.

It actually got so hot last night that Charlian had to go nude with the rest of the men (and most of the women) to stay cool. And for some reason Aleshia hadn't mined.

If anything Charlian wondered if it had made Aleshia work harder so they could both go back to the tent sooner. Sadly (for both of them) by the time they went back, Aleshia went straight to sleep. Charlian was a tat disappointed there.

But he was more than pleased when he managed to read that magazine article on the Ingnic Empire and the findings of their objects in the modern day Elven territory.

In fact, other historians had discovered a strange dagger-like tooth three times the size of a normal man. Charlian was a bit taller than the average man, but he really hoped that it was proof of Megaragons in the Elven territories.

Only providing more evidence for their idea, or

at this point it was more of a scientific theory.

The sounds of the expedition crew talking, laughing and playing card games with each other started to slow down as they saw Aleshia in her sexy tan-coloured shirt, trousers and her tight boots.

Charlian just stared at her for a moment, admiring her stunning beauty. He really was so lucky to have such a stunning woman in his life. He was never going to take her for granted, not even for a second.

Then Octon moved slightly and Charlian kissed her fiery orange scales, and she smiled. Octon was another amazing woman in his life.

Sure she couldn't fit into the mess tent, pyramid or cave. But she was still special. Without her the missing team with the Megaragon skeleton might never have been found and rescued, it was really all because of Octon that they had managed to solve the mystery of the fall of the Ingnic Empire.

"Thank you," Charlian whispered as he stroked Octon's snout.

"Sure Boss," Octon said, "I always got ya back,"

"Professor Charlian," Aleshia said formally.

Charlian turned around and went over to his amazing wife and held her hand as they both stared at all 30 members of the crew. Everyone here was so pleased, happy and really wanted to be here. Charlian just loved that.

He really did.

"Thank you everyone," Aleshia said. "You have

all done amazing. Me and Charlian… cannot express how grateful we are,"

Someone went to stand up but Aleshia waved him to sit back down. Charlian didn't doubt for a second his wife had asked him to stand up at that moment.

Charlian smiled. "We honestly didn't expect to get this much done so soon. But now we believe we know what happened to the Ingnic Empire and the Masked One,"

Everyone smiled and muttered amongst themselves. Charlian noticed the massive amount of energy and excitement in the air.

He couldn't blame them.

"The Ingnic Empire was formed four thousand years ago," Aleshia said, "and they quickly started to integrate different tribes, countries and even one or two mini-empires into themselves,"

Everyone nodded.

"So," Charlian said, "when they integrated a country around two hundred kilometres southeast of here. There was an influx of new religions and beliefs and trade into the empire,"

Aleshia started shaking with excitement. "So the Ingnic Empire and the Royal Family had to decide what beliefs to allow to be mixed into the folklore of the Ingnics. They dismissed most of them but there was one belief these newly Integrated people wouldn't allow to leave,"

"The Masked One stories," Jesscio said.

Now Charlian was starting to get extremely excited!

Charlian nodded. "Correct. So the Royal Family decided to test out these so-called stories,"

Aleshia started talking with her hands. Charlian took a few steps away. He knew how dangerous she could get.

"So," Aleshia said, "the Empire got five test subjects of the people. Then they conducted some experiments on them. The first three died of natural causes,"

"The fourth died of insanity or something like that. But we believe he had a vision of the Masked One," Charlian said, "Then the fifth is a lot more interesting,"

Aleshia jumped up and down with excitement. Charlian was never going to blame her. This was amazing stuff.

"The Royal Family must have learnt of something that made them a lot more careful about their studies," Aleshia said.

"They probably," Charlian said, "found out the newly integrated country would try anything to keep their stories. So they probably tried to stop the Royal Family or make them believe it,"

Charlian watched as everyone's eyes widened.

"Making the Royal Family of the Empire," Aleshia said, "decide to create a double-blind subject in their study. So they created a fake body by carefully wrapping up parchment into the shape of a body," added some mixture of honey and lemons and rotten meat to make it look and feel real,"

Charlian smiled. This was the really clever bit.

"Afterwards the Royal Family," Aleshia said, "placed that fake body in the cave and nailed it to the ceiling like they did with the others,"

Aleshia accidentally hit him with her crazy fast hands.

Charlian stepped away from the hands of death. "But in reality, they put the body of flesh and blood in the coffin in the pyramid with a Guardian to watch over the body,"

Everyone muttered amongst themselves.

"Oh professors," Carl said, "but where is the Guardian and what about that massive skeleton?"

Charlian smiled. He had been waiting for that. "You see last night Octon went back to the Megaragon skull and took a… what do you call it?"

Octon stomped on over. "I call it a Drag-Dragon Taste. I licked that creature's bones all over, ya know,"

Charlian watched Aleshia try to suppress her laughter. She failed.

"And Octon found," Charlian said, "that the Megaragon is definitely three thousand years old and that is around the time the man in the coffin was eaten,"

"But Professor Aleshia said the man died around three thousand years ago," Jesscio said.

Aleshia smiled. "Well that is where things get

even more interesting. Last night me and Charlian finished going through the parchment pages that you kindly unpicked for us. We found something strange,"

"What?" everyone asked on the edge of their seats.

Charlian just looked at Aleshia and she nodded.

Charlian cocked his head for a moment. "We found the Ingnic Empire had magic users and most of the parchment was written in their black blood. The words were a spell that stopped the flesh from rotting until the body was attacked and eaten,"

"Oh professors," Carl said, "so the man died four thousand years ago. But the magic kept him physically alive as far as your bone test was concerned for another thousand years,"

Charlian nodded. "And the Royal Family allowed the stories to be maintained for that first thousand years because their studies were still on-going,"

Aleshia waved her hands around rapidly. "And!"

Charlian took a few steps away.

"And when the Megaragon attacked the Guardian. The creature tasted the Guardian. So we never found him and then the creature attacked the coffin. Eating some of the fifth man,"

Some of the crew still looked a bit suspicious. "And some of the wrappings suggested that Megaragons were magically sensitive. So the creatures would only attack things without symbols or runes to warn them away,"

Everyone nodded.

Charlian was amazed how great it felt to have solved everything. And this is what he loved about history and exploring the past.

Because it was always, always surprising and filled with adventure.

And as Charlian looked around at each of the brilliant people in the mess tent, he knew he was never going to stop exploring, discovering and uncovering the secrets of history.

It was just part of who he was. And he always wanted to be around with his sexy wife, amazing Octon and his damn wonderful crew.

All of those people Charlian was nothing without, and he knew it, and he damn well loved each and every one of them for it.

CHAPTER 18

As the stunningly beautiful sun started to set in the boiling hot desert, Aleshia just sat in the canvas mess tent watching everyone outside playing a massive game of football in the sand.

All the men were topless and the women were just in bras, and realised she loved leaving the university. She had allowed them to dress so-called inappropriately because it was far too hot for them to wear clothes anymore.

Even now with the sun setting, Aleshia was still sweating and she was wishing the heat would stop. So she had no problem if the crew wanted to be cool and enjoy themselves.

They deserved it.

And Aleshia truly, truly believed that. For the past two days, her amazing crew had worked flat out to help her and Charlian with the expedition and finding out what had happened to the Ingnic Empire.

Even the sounds of them laughing, playing and having fun was… so strangely touching and it made Aleshia feel alive and like she was meant to be here.

Watching all the crew play together was like watching her family get along.

Because that was what they were. Her crew was her family. A family she damn well loved.

The air smelt so dry and warm and deadly. But every so often there was a stunningly cool breeze that Aleshia just hung onto because it was so great.

And in all honesty that was why Aleshia loved the Ingnic Empire. Because it wasn't just another civilization that had grown into a force to be reckoned with by starting in some wet land near to a river so they could easily grow food.

No. The Ingnic Empire defied logic. They had created one of the largest empires in history from this very spot, in the middle of nowhere in the middle of a horribly hot desert.

No one else could do that in the past, present or future. But somehow these absolutely brilliant people had, and they had made sure to leave a mark on history.

It wasn't until later in the afternoon after a nap that she had explained to everyone why the Ingnic Empire never fell into the gas cave or chamber that the Megaragon skeleton had created.

It was too simple really.

It turned out the Ingnic empire always created a so-called Natural place in their territories. It was actually Charlian when he reread that magazine article had told her about it. Apparently the Elves had given the Ingnics a small area of land and they refused to build anything on a one kilometre stretch of it. Because the Royal Family believed in preserving the natural environment.

So it just so happened that their preserved chunk of earth was right where that Megaragon skeleton was. Aleshia had no doubt the Royal Family knew about the skeleton.

She didn't know how. She just knew that they knew about it. It was the only thing that made any sense.

And that was why they never discovered the skeleton (at least publicly).

Aleshia felt her stomach start to flip and fill with butterflies as she started to imagine what life was like in the Empire. But all those ideas quickly faded when she remembered when she told everyone how the Ingnic Empire fell.

That was the entire reason they were there.

After everything Aleshia had learnt about the Empire in the past two days and how clever they were and how strangely they collapsed. Aleshia and Charlian and everyone had come to only one conclusion.

The empire didn't fall two thousand years ago.

It sounded strange when the crew had first suggested it, but after thinking about it for a few hours, Aleshia realised she had to agree.

The history books were wrong about the fall of the Megaragons, so why not the fall of the Empire?

And if her decades of studying history taught her

anything, it was that massive empires never ever just collapsed overnight. There were always, without a single exception, smaller factors that were reported and recorded that led up to the fall of an empire.

Aleshia had no doubt it had happened here. In the next few hundred years after the official fall of the Ingnics, Aleshia had read about various wars of independence, plagues and even some mass famines that wiped out entire countries.

But there was one thing no historian could ever figure out.

What country or empire did these countries gain independence from?

But now after two amazing days of exploring, discovering and uncovering secrets, Aleshia just knew that she had figured it out.

So no, the Ingnic Empire didn't just suddenly fall after two thousand amazing years. It fell a lot later after famines, plagues and some wars of independence.

And that was exactly what she would be writing in her report.

Yet there was still one thing bothering her. After everything that had happened at Mount Flame with her possession, attacking her own husband and almost causing the end of the Realm, she had come here not knowing what drove her anymore.

She still didn't know what drove her.

Then the sound of the crew screaming in happiness as one side scored an apparent *legendary* goal that made Aleshia look at them and she really looked. She especially stared at her stunning sexy husband who was topless, revealing his utterly amazing six-pack and body.

And Aleshia smiled as she realised they were what truly drove her.

Sure the exploring, discovering and uncovering secrets and history drove her, they were things that made her want to keep going out on these expeditions.

Yet it was the amazing people she worked with that made her really want to come out here.

It was the people like Jessico and the crew with such a passion that she loved. It was the people like Carl with their neediness that came from wanting to do well that she loved, and it was the people like her husband who supported her that she truly, truly loved.

So as Aleshia sat there staring at her family. She just wanted to be with them and celebrate. Sure there was still a hell of a lot of excavating, report writing and paying to do but that really was tomorrow's problem.

Right now Aleshia had her family to see.

Aleshia got up and just walked over to her family and started playing football with them.

And as Aleshia played, had fun and just got filled with energy, she realised there was nowhere else she would rather be in the entire world.

And she was perfectly happy with that.

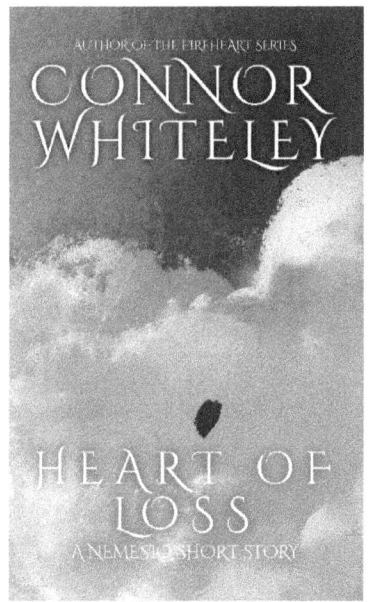

GET YOUR FREE AND EXCLUSIVE SHORT STORY NOW! LEARN ABOUT NEMESIO'S PAST!

https://www.subscribepage.com/fireheart

Keep up to date with exclusive deals on Connor Whiteley's Books, as well as the latest news about new releases and so much more!

Sign up for the Grab a Book and Chill Monthly newsletter, and you'll get one **FREE** ebook just for signing up: Agents of The Emperor Collection.

Sign Up Now!

https://dl.bookfunnel.com/f4p5xkprbk

About the author:

Connor Whiteley is the author of over 60 books in the sci-fi fantasy, nonfiction psychology and books for writer's genre and he is a Human Branding Speaker and Consultant.

He is a passionate warhammer 40,000 reader, psychology student and author.

Who narrates his own audiobooks and he hosts The Psychology World Podcast.

All whilst studying Psychology at the University of Kent, England.

Also, he was a former Explorer Scout where he gave a speech to the Maltese President in August 2018 and he attended Prince Charles' 70th Birthday Party at Buckingham Palace in May 2018.

Plus, he is a self-confessed coffee lover!

OTHER SHORT STORIES BY CONNOR WHITELEY

Blade of The Emperor

Arbiter's Truth

The Bloodied Rose

Asmodia's Wrath

Heart of A Killer

Emissary of Blood

Computation of Battle

Old One's Wrath

Puppets and Masters

Ship of Plague

Interrogation

Edge of Failure

One Way Choice

Acceptable Losses

Balance of Power

Good Idea At The Time

Escape Plan

Escape In The Hesitation

Inspiration In Need

Singing Warriors

Dragon Coins

Dragon Tea

Dragon Rider

Knowledge is Power

Killer of Polluters

THE MASKED ONE

Climate of Death
Sacrifice of the Soul
Heart of The Flesheater
Heart of The Regent
Heart of The Standing
Feline of The Lost
Heart of The Story
The Family Mailing Affair
Defining Criminality
The Martian Affair
A Cheating Affair
The Little Café Affair
Mountain of Death
Prisoner's Fight
Claws of Death
Bitter Air
Honey Hunt
Blade On A Train
City of Fire
Awaiting Death
Poison In The Candy Cane
Christmas Innocence
You Better Watch Out
Christmas Theft
Trouble In Christmas
Smell of The Lake
Problem In A Car

Theft, Past and Team
Embezzler In The Room
A Strange Way To Go
A Horrible Way To Go
Ann Awful Way To Go
An Old Way To Go
A Fishy Way To Go
A Pointy Way To Go
A High Way To Go
A Fiery Way To Go
A Glassy Way To Go
A Chocolatey Way To Go
Kendra Detective Mystery Collection Volume 1
Kendra Detective Mystery Collection Volume 2
Stealing A Chance At Freedom
Glassblowing and Death
Theft of Independence
Cookie Thief
Marble Thief
Book Thief
Art Thief

Other books by Connor Whiteley:

The Fireheart Fantasy Series

Heart of Fire

Heart of Lies

Heart of Prophecy

Heart of Bones

Heart of Fate

City of Assassins (Urban Fantasy)

City of Death

City of Marytrs

City of Pleasure

City of Power

Agents of The Emperor

Return of The Ancient Ones

Vigilance

Angels of Fire

The Garro Series- Fantasy/Sci-fi

GARRO: GALAXY'S END

GARRO: RISE OF THE ORDER

GARRO: END TIMES

GARRO: SHORT STORIES

GARRO: COLLECTION

GARRO: HERESY

GARRO: FAITHLESS
GARRO: DESTROYER OF WORLDS
GARRO: COLLECTIONS BOOK 4-6
GARRO: MISTRESS OF BLOOD
GARRO: BEACON OF HOPE
GARRO: END OF DAYS

Winter Series- Fantasy Trilogy Books
WINTER'S COMING
WINTER'S HUNT
WINTER'S REVENGE
WINTER'S DISSENSION

Bettie English Private Eye Series
A Very Private Woman
The Russian Case

Miscellaneous:
RETURN
FREEDOM
SALVATION
Reflection of Mount Flame
The Masked One
The Great Deer

THE MASKED ONE

All books in 'An Introductory Series':
BIOLOGICAL PSYCHOLOGY 3RD EDITION
COGNITIVE PSYCHOLOGY THIRD EDITION
SOCIAL PSYCHOLOGY- 3RD EDITION
ABNORMAL PSYCHOLOGY 3RD EDITION
PSYCHOLOGY OF RELATIONSHIPS- 3RD EDITION
DEVELOPMENTAL PSYCHOLOGY 3RD EDITION
HEALTH PSYCHOLOGY
RESEARCH IN PSYCHOLOGY
A GUIDE TO MENTAL HEALTH AND TREATMENT AROUND THE WORLD- A GLOBAL LOOK AT DEPRESSION
FORENSIC PSYCHOLOGY
THE FORENSIC PSYCHOLOGY OF THEFT, BURGLARY AND OTHER CRIMES AGAINST PROPERTY
CRIMINAL PROFILING: A FORENSIC PSYCHOLOGY GUIDE TO FBI PROFILING AND GEOGRAPHICAL AND STATISTICAL PROFILING.
CLINICAL PSYCHOLOGY
FORMULATION IN PSYCHOTHERAPY

PERSONALITY PSYCHOLOGY AND INDIVIDUAL DIFFERENCES
CLINICAL PSYCHOLOGY REFLECTIONS VOLUME 1
CLINICAL PSYCHOLOGY REFLECTIONS VOLUME 2
CULT PSYCHOLOGY
Police Psychology

Companion guides:
BIOLOGICAL PSYCHOLOGY 2ND EDITION WORKBOOK
COGNITIVE PSYCHOLOGY 2ND EDITION WORKBOOK
SOCIOCULTURAL PSYCHOLOGY 2ND EDITION WORKBOOK
ABNORMAL PSYCHOLOGY 2ND EDITION WORKBOOK
PSYCHOLOGY OF HUMAN RELATIONSHIPS 2ND EDITION WORKBOOK
HEALTH PSYCHOLOGY WORKBOOK
FORENSIC PSYCHOLOGY WORKBOOK

www.ingramcontent.com/pod-product-compliance
Lightning Source LLC
LaVergne TN
LVHW012114070526
838202LV00056B/5733